This SCRIBBLERS

book belongs to:

....

This edition published in Great Britain in MMXVIII
by Scribblers, an imprint of
The Salariya Book Company Ltd
25 Marlborough Place,
Brighton BN1 1UB
www.salariya.com

SALARIYA
SCRIBO   BOOK HOUSE   SCRIBBLERS

© Editions Langue Au Chat - BELGIUM
English language © The Salariya Book Company Ltd MMXVIII

HB ISBN-13: 978-1-912006-81-6

1 3 5 7 9 8 6 4 2

A CIP catalogue record for this book is
available from the British Library.

Printed and bound in China

Printed on paper from sustainable sources

Visit
www.salariya.com
for our online catalogue and
free fun stuff.

Fabien Öckto Lambert is a graphic
designer, illustrator, and writer of children's
books. He lives in Nantes in France.

Odd Dog

Fabien Öckto Lambert

SCRIBBLERS

a SALARIYA *imprint*

Mr Rogers has lots and lots of dogs.

He has long dogs, rectangular dogs, dogs as big as horses, and dogs so small that they're almost invisible.

Mr Rogers is waiting for his new dog
to be delivered. This dog will be the best,
the biggest and the strongest dog.
It will be a dog with real woofability!

*T*he crate has arrived and Mr Rogers eases open the lid. But what will he find inside?

Oh, what a surprise! What
tiny feet! What a long snout!
What a shade of green!
Oh yes, Mr Rogers is very
impressed by this mighty and
unusual dog.

"We'll call him Barney,"
says Mr Rogers. "I can't wait
to take him out for a walk."

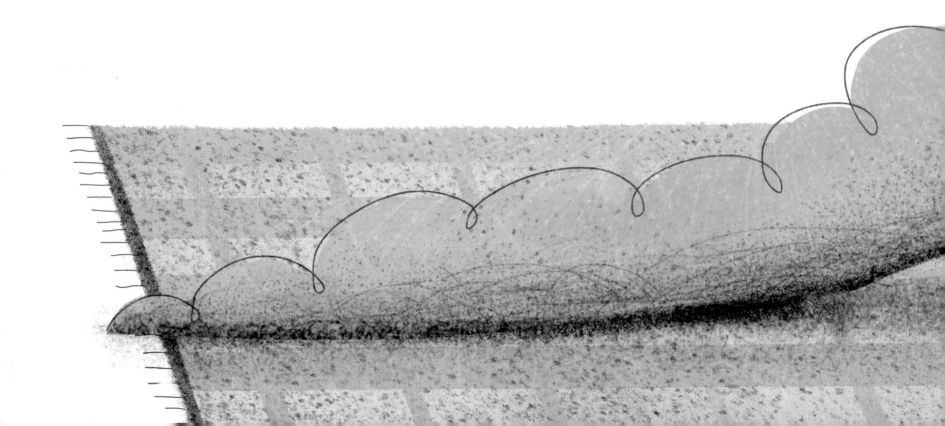

*B*arney is hopeless at fetching the paper.

When Mr Rogers plays tennis,
Barney won't run for the ball.

He chews the racket instead.

*M*r Rogers and Barney make an impressive pair as they walk down the street with their heads in the air.

"*T*hat's an odd dog!" the baker calls out.
"Without a doubt, I've never seen a dog
with such a long snout!"

But before the baker knows
it - gulp! Oh my gosh, this dog
Barney has gobbled up his shop!

Mr Rogers and Barney make an impressive pair as they walk down the street with their heads in the air.

"*T*hat's an odd dog!" the pastry shop owner calls out. "Without a doubt, I've never seen a dog with such a long snout!"

Barney stretches his jaws wide and takes a giant bite. Gulp! Oh my gosh, this dog Barney has eaten the pastry maker's shop! It's too late, too late. Barney is already licking his lips.

Mr Rogers and Barney make an
impressive pair as they walk down
the street with their heads in the air.

"*T*hat's an odd dog!" the florist calls out.
"Without a doubt, I've never seen a dog
   with such a long snout!"

*B*arney opens his jaws wide and once again his teeth go crunch. Down go the tulips, the cacti and everything else. Gulp! Oh my gosh, he's eaten the lot!

The shop owners are very angry. All of their bread, cakes, and flowers have gone.

*B*arney has even munched on a watering can and chewed through an umbrella!

After his enjoyable walk, Mr Rogers wonders why the shop owners are so cross.

"What's that you say?" asks Mr Rogers.
"My dog has eaten everything up?
Hmm…What can I do to sort this out?"

"Wait! I have an idea," cries Mr Rogers with a smile.

"*W*e'll enter Barney into the Greatest Cake Eater In The World Contest."

*B*arney wins the competition hands down and becomes a global celebrity.

People come from around the world to see Barney. The dog with the tiny feet. The dog with the long snout. The dog with the greenish hue.

A very impressive, very unusual, very odd dog. If he is in fact a dog at all?

*O*h no, not again!

*T*he florist's budgie has
mysteriously disappeared...

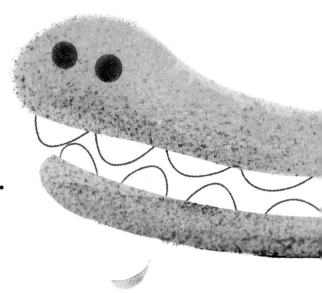

BARNEY?!!